HOPE

HOPE

by Isabell Monk
illustrations by Janice Lee Porter

Carolrhoda Books, Inc./Minneapolis

Every summer I spend at least one weekend in the country with my mama's aunt Poogee. The instant I step out of our car, Aunt Poogee scoops me up in her arms and says, "Mmmm, I could just eat you up." I think Aunt Poogee holds all the love in the world inside her and lets it out bit by bit through the twinkle in her eye.

The summer before second grade (I'm in sixth grade now), I spent a weekend at Aunt Poogee's that I'll always remember. Early Saturday morning, we got into Aunt Poogee's pink Cadillac, which she won for selling more Fancy Mae cosmetics than any other lady in three states. We drove along the river to the open-air market.

I always loved the big, crowded marketplace. Aunt Poogee saw lots of her friends there. First we ran into Mr. Stewart, my favorite. He has a smile like a picket fence. Aunt Poogee calls him Stew-pot because of his big potbelly. Like always, he had some cherry licorice for me and, of course, a smile.

Then I met Miss Teacup Hill, a woman about Aunt Poogee's age—and my size. Aunt Poogee said, "Her real name is Thelma, but folks call her Teacup because when she was born, she was so small her mama used a teacup for a cradle."

All of a sudden, across the whole market came a sound only a steam whistle could make: "Pru-dence, Prudence Nivens?" Aunt Poogee's real name is Prudence. My Grandpa Jack, who is her big brother, could only say Poogee when he was little. It stuck.

"Well, long time no see, girl!" the human
steam whistle said.

"So you came home, Violet? You don't look a
day older!" Aunt Poogee said as they hugged
each other. Miss Violet and Aunt Poogee grew
up together, but Miss Violet moved away. She
comes back every few years to visit.

They chatted on about who had died, who had
married, who had divorced, and who had had
new babies. Then Aunt Poogee put her arm
around my shoulder and said, "Violet, I'll bet
you can't guess whose baby this is."

Miss Violet looked over her glasses and down her nose at me. She even gestured for me to turn around. Then she declared, "Prudence, this child doesn't favor a soul in your family."

"She's Eve's little girl. You remember Eve, don't you? My brother Jack's daughter?" Aunt Poogee said.

"Oh my, yessss," Miss Violet said suspiciously. "Well, she sure enough has her mama's big brown eyes." Miss Violet couldn't take her eyes off me. She leaned into Aunt Poogee and in a low voice said, "My goodness, Prudence, is the child mixed?"

Aunt Poogee put her hand up like a traffic cop, rolled her eyes, set her mouth, and in a razor-sharp voice said, "Violet, what on earth do you think?" After that they said their good-byes, and we finished our shopping and headed home.

The ride home was quiet, the most quiet ride I can remember. Finally I asked, "What did Miss Violet mean, 'Is the child mixed?'"

Aunt Poogee stroked my head with one hand and said, "Baby, don't you pay Violet no never mind." But I did.

All the way home I thought about what Miss
Violet had said. All through my afternoon
snack, all through helping Aunt Poogee snap the
fresh green beans, all through dinner, all through
brushing my teeth, and even as I said my
prayers, I could not stop hearing Miss Violet say,
"My goodness, Prudence, is the child mixed?"

But when I heard Aunt Poogee's slippers
clip-clop, clip-clop, clip-clopping down the
hall toward me, all thoughts of Miss Violet went
clip-clop, right out of my head.

It was time for my favorite part of the weekend. Just before I get into bed, Aunt Poogee comes into the room, sits in the big old rocking chair near the window, rocks me on her lap, and tells me stories about our family.

Sometimes it's the story of her and Grandpa Jack when they were my age and lived on a farm. They could never get those flying-frying chickens out of the cherry tree for Great-grandma Nellie to cook up for Sunday dinner.

Sometimes it's the story of how she had to scrub my mama from head to toe with tomato juice after Mama found a black kitty with a white stripe down her back. The kitty turned out to be a skunk.

Sometimes it's just quiet humming and the sound of Aunt Poogee's sturdy heartbeat to tell the night's tale.

That night, as Aunt Poogee rocked, she asked
me, "Would you like to know how you got your
name?" The story had never been about me
before. I was so excited that all I could do was
nod my head "yes." In her best bedtime voice,
Aunt Poogee began my story.

You have your mother's beautiful brown eyes. You have the noble shape of your father's face. Your skin is the color of delicious things, like a perfect cup of cocoa, my special golden-fried chicken, or the apricot jam you helped me make last summer.

Baby, when people like Violet look at you, they think you are made only of what they can see. But I know what it truly took to make Hope.

It took the faith of your daddy's immigrant great, great, great, great-grandparents to be true to their dreams.

It took the faith of your mama's enslaved great, great, great, great-grandparents to know that a better day was coming.

It took the faith of your Grandpa Jack and Grandma Jane to stand up in the face of hatred, fear, and ignorance.

WE WILL MARCH AS LONG AS WE CAN and DEMAND THE RIGHTS OF Everyman

It took the faith of your Grandpa Vince and
Grandma Kate to teach others that knowledge is
freedom and should be free.

And most important was the faith of your very own mama and daddy to look forward to a future where you will be proud to be part of a race that is simply "human."

So when someone asks, "My goodness, is the child mixed?"
you can say in a clear voice, "Yes, I am generations of faith
'mixed' with lots of love! I AM HOPE!"

With those words, Aunt Poogee put me into bed, kissed me with a butterfly kiss, and said, "Good night, Hope."

That weekend, I realized how lucky I am to have Aunt Poogee. Her stories tell me where I'm from and help me to get where I'm going. But her stories are not for me to keep—they are for me to share.

A special thanks to Sheila Livingston for her belief in me, Amy Gelman for taking a chance on me, Janice Lee Porter for giving Hope *a face, and Melissa Warden for pulling it all together—I.M.*

This book is dedicated to Senait Judge Yoakam, Jacqueline Nicole Hodson, and all children "mixed" with love—I.M.

To my Aunt Boots, with love—J.L.P.

Carolrhoda Books, Inc., c/o The Lerner Publishing Group
241 First Avenue North, Minneapolis, MN 55401 U.S.A.

Website address: www.lernerbooks.com

Library of Congress Cataloging-in-Publication Data

Monk, Isabell.
    Hope / by Isabell Monk : illustrations by Janice Lee Porter.
        p.   cm.
    Summary: During a visit with her great-aunt, a young girl learns the story behind her name and learns to feel proud of her biracial heritage.
        ISBN 1–57505–230–X (alk. paper)
    [1. Racially mixed peoples—Fiction. 2. Great-aunts—Fiction. 3. Names, Personal—Fiction.] I. Porter, Janice Lee, ill. II. Title
PZ7.M75115Ho 1999
[E]—dc21   98-16339

Manufactured in the United States of America
1 2 3 4 5 6 – JR – 04 03 02 01 00 99